Hutton C Hamilton

Martha

Hutton C Hamilton

Martha

ISBN/EAN: 9783742812384

Manufactured in Europe, USA, Canada, Australia, Japa

Cover: Foto ©Andreas Hilbeck / pixelio.de

Manufactured and distributed by brebook publishing software
(www.brebook.com)

Hutton C Hamilton

Martha

MARTHA ❧ BY HUTTON C. HAMILTON ❧ ❧

NEW YORK AND LONDON ❧ G. P. PUTNAM'S SONS ❧ ❧ ❧

Printed and Bound by
The Knickerbocker Press, New York
G. P. PUTNAM'S SONS

CHARACTERS.

RICHARD MARDYKE.

TOM MADDEN.

COUNT REFSTEIN.

ROMVERTON.

PEPE.

GERALDINE.

MARTHA.

MRS. ROMVERTON.

MRS. SCHREINER.

NITA.

DOCTOR, DETECTIVE, SOLDIERS, GUARDS, ETC.

MARTHA.

I.

Sitting-room, Richard Mardyke's house, Spanish Pyrenees. Stage divided, showing in- and out-side of house. Two windows, back, large; one window, side (in partition dividing room from garden), small. Door by latter, leading outside. House stands on cliff overlooking valley (back), and the Mountain of the Maladetta in the distance. A porch and stair (outside) lead up to Richard Mardyke's library. . . . Fire burning. Curtain rises, showing Richard Mardyke by small table at window, reading.

RICHARD MARDYKE

Putting down book

Three weeks, and nothing from Durfee yet ! . . . Strange he should be so long ! . . . (*Lights a match and his pipe.*) . . . I suppose he's off somewhere. Editors are incorrigible. . . . I'll write before the next manuscript goes. . . . How clear the air is ! . . . I can see the light on the stream down the valley. . . . But there's a feeling I don't like in the air. . . . Just as well perhaps I did n't go across country to-night. . . . One grows weather-wise. . . . After three years. . . . Three years ! (*Rising.*) I begin to feel like a part of the landscape. . . . I wonder if the old mountain would miss me. . . . Madden says I'm a fool to stay here. . . . May be I am. . . . But I stay. (*Goes to window, back.*) . . . Curious cloud ! . . . Does he think her death will drive her face away from the old places ? . . . Madden's an ass ! . . . (*Pulls at pipe.*) . . . Damn the pipe ! . . . (*Re-lights it.*) Ah ! here comes postman Pepe crawling up the hill. Poor old devil ! I suppose if it were not for the *aguadiente* I corrupt him with he 'd curse me with the help of every saint in Spain. . . . Belief lives on hard fare here. —But it lives. . . . Murky weather ! . . . Sticky ! . . . (*Goes to door and opens it. Enter* PEPE.)   Well, Pepe, muddy tramping, eh ?

PEPE

Ay, Señor ; (*shifting bag around*) and it 'll be worse to-night.

RICHARD MARDYKE

Yes ; I am afraid so.   How are you in the valley ?

PEPE

Bad, Señor, bad !   There 'll be wind. (*Hands letters.*)   Pardo's place went over last year.

RICHARD MARDYKE

I remember. (*Glancing over them.*) Send your wife and children up here if there is trouble.

PEPE

Thank you, Señor. God bless you! Did the Señor see the light along the edge of the snow? It looks bad—very bad. I know when it is not far off.—I know.

RICHARD MARDYKE

Go back, Pepe, and get something warm from Nita. She's waiting for you.

PEPE

Thank you, Señor. It's a hard walk for me now. Once it was nothing. The mountain looks but a league away! (*He goes, passing window, back.*)

RICHARD MARDYKE

The fools make no provisions until the last moment. I'll go down myself and have a look later. (*Reads letters.*) Trover, Vance, Dudley (*returns to study-table by window, back, and sits down. Reads*), Deggs & Whiffin! (*Opening.*) The afflictions of lawyers seem to be their names. . . . We beg to inform . . . adjustment? . . . the late Tobias Hurd? A good deal of fuss because old uncle Hurd did n't divide his two millions in the middle, but would have ten thousand a year more on my side than on Geraldine's. . . . Uncles (*takes another letter*) are such— . . . (*Stops.*) I suppose Geraldine is a woman now. . . . Just seventeen when I left. Poor little sister . . . and mother. (*Takes out photographs from desk. Looks at them, kisses them, puts his head down on his arms for a moment. Recovering himself and tearing open other letters.*) Dear Sir: You are herewith informed that your annual dues (*throws it down.*) . . . Clubs! (*Takes another.*) Ah! a line from Durfee at last! (*Reads.*) Your last bundle reached me on my return from Edinburgh. Have just read it myself. Keep up the vein, old man. You are sweeping all before you. Will follow your plan, which is best, as to publication and send you proofs. Am much over-worked since return here. When do you come out of your shell? Much as I want to see you, don't come if it is to spoil your present run of ideas. You see I have an *eye to the prophets*—you remember my old Scotch yarn. Yours, Durfee. (*Looking up.*) So he thinks it's a success! . . . Well, so do I. . . . What it

cost me! I owe it all to her. . . .
Driving me on. . . . (*Opens another.*)
Ah, Madden! (*Reads.*) You are
surprised to hear from me here—
Where? (*Turns letter over.*) Bayonne!—
as you know how I loathe this sort of
place. All the South of France has its
terrors. It is for another, as you may
suppose, I am come. Two nights ago
Refstein joined me— . . . (*Looking up.*)
Refstein!— . . . to my utter amazement,
in *St. Jean de Lux*, and insists on my
taking him to you, as he speaks no Spanish— . . . Here! He here!— . . . I do
so in fear and trembling, not knowing
whether you are at work or not; you may
expect us at any moment. I have just
seen Durfee. He is radiant. Says you
come out soon with a new piece. Do I
bring an unwelcome visitor? He has
something important to talk about. I

suspect, but say nothing. (*Looks up.*) Important ! (*Walks to window.*) I should think Madden would have better sense than to bring him here. (*Enter* NITA.) What is it, Nita ? (*Annoyed.*)

NITA

I came to close the windows, Señor. The wind is so strong, and Pepe says——

RICHARD MARDYKE

Pepe 's croaking again ! Never mind the windows now. (*Wind moans outside and blows papers violently.* NITA *hesitates.*) Oh, well, close them. (NITA *does so. Sound of rumbling wheels outside.* RICHARD MARDYKE *takes out his watch and looks at it.*) What 's that ! Nita ? (*Aside.*) It 's too late for the coach now !

NITA

It must be the Pons coach, Señor. Pepe says it 's very late to-day. There was an accident he thought. It ought to have been here long ago.

RICHARD MARDYKE

I should think so! An accident! (*Looking at watch*) four hours at least! I wonder when I ought to expect them. (*Glances at letter*) . . . Just like Madden! expects me to divine his arrival by intuition. (*Rattle of wheels near and sound of coach stopping.* NITA *goes to window, back, and looks out.*)

NITA

Yes, Señor; the Pons coach. I can see the yellow on the wheels though

they 're mostly hid with the mud. The
Tartana from Barbastro came in an hour
ago . . . And there 's José and Mariano
and the others . . . And José's got a
skin of wine. There ! He is holding
it up now and they are all laughing,
and oh !—here are two gentlemen coming with Pepe—he 's carrying their
things—and one of them is laughing and
pointing up here.

RICHARD MARDYKE

What 's that ? (*Goes to window.*) By
George it 's so ! . . . and, yes . . .
it is . . . of course it is. It 's Madden,
and (*frowning*) Refstein. (*Goes to
door and opens it. After a pause they
appear. Shaking hands with* MADDEN.)
I 'm so glad to see you again, old man.
Been well ? (*Turns more formally to*
REFSTEIN *and shakes hands.*) I hardly

expected you to follow your letter so closely. Why did n't you bring it yourselves?

REFSTEIN

Did you just get it?

RICHARD MARDYKE

It came in on the Southern coach an hour ago.

MADDEN

Laughing

Quite enough. Keeps the ball of surprise rolling, you know. But I say, my dear fellow, if we had n't been delayed four hours you 'd have had it two hours after we arrived.

REFSTEIN

Three.

MADDEN

Three is it? (*Looking at* RICHARD MARDYKE *musingly.*)—Oh, damn the time. How are you?

RICHARD MARDYKE

Did you ever know me ill? But come in. When did you leave?

MADDEN

Leave where, Paris, America, London, St. Petersburg? Just look at that fire, Refstein!

RICHARD MARDYKE

New York, of course.

MADDEN

Have n't you heard from Geraldine? Came over with her and your mother—— same boat, *Majestic.* Left them in Paris trying on clothes. Shut up, Refstein (*as he starts to speak.*)

RICHARD MARDYKE

In Paris! Geraldine in Paris! And my mother!

REFSTEIN

Did n't you know it?

MADDEN

Good Lord, have you so hermitized yourself out of countenance with your own flesh and blood! Why, my dear fellow, it 's perfectly lawless! . . . But I say (*throwing off his coat*) I 'm cold and damp (*leans over fire.*) Now you know (*making significant gestures to* RICHARD MARDYKE.)

Richard Mardyke

Yes, of course. (*Aside.*) . . . All of them in Paris! Strange! (*Goes to closet and gets out bottle of brandy and glasses.*) Here, Nita, the water. (*To* Madden.) When did they come?

Nita
Who is just carrying out satchel with Pepe

Yes, sir. (*Disappears.*)

Madden

Don't forget the sugar, old man.

Richard Mardyke
Handing it mechanically

I 've had no word.

Madden

Naturally enough, as you forbade any letters whatever. Why, my dear fellow,

you 've been shut in by the strictest
quarantine in Europe.

RICHARD MARDYKE

But why are they here? What brings
them across at this time? Is anything
wrong? (*Anxiously.*) Is my mother——?

MADDEN

All well—nothing to disturb you.

REFSTEIN

But you had my letter?

RICHARD MARDYKE

Your letter? (*Surprised.*) What
letter?—no.

REFSTEIN

My letter sent from New York telling
you all about my plans.

RICHARD MARDYKE

Your plans—what plans ?

REFSTEIN

Why my——

MADDEN

Refstein, be quiet. (*Aside.*) The devil !
. . . Where 's that water ? Ah ! (NITA
brings it.—He holds brandy over REFSTEIN'S
glass.) Here, Refstein, say when.

REFSTEIN

There.   There !

MADDEN

To Richard Mardyke, as Nita retires

Is that the best you can do in this land
of eyes and ankles ? I swear ! (*Aside.*)
We 've got to go all over it again ! (*In a*

low voice aside to REFSTEIN.)   We 're in for
it, Refstein.

REFSTEIN
Also in low voice

So it seems.

MADDEN
To Richard Mardyke, pointing after Nita

I say. . . no others?

RICHARD MARDYKE
Laughing

No.   You don't know her.

MADDEN

Thank God !   Where 's the sugar ?

REFSTEIN

Here.   (*Pushes it.*)

RICHARD MARDYKE

Will you tell me the news?
(MADDEN *pours out large glass of brandy ;
carefully measures two spoonfuls of water
into it.*)
Nothing like water for flavor. . . .
News! My dear fellow, there is n't any.

RICHARD MARDYKE

Have you brought me nothing? . . .
no letters? (*Aside.*) What are they
concealing?

MADDEN

Everybody 's well. How the devil do
you get things here in winter?

RICHARD MARDYKE

We don't. We follow the example of
the laborious ant and lay in a plentiful
supply in the good season. I 'm comfort-

able enough here. It 's the warmest house in Spain, I believe. No Sevillian marble floors for me. But Geraldine——

MADDEN

Now see here, I 'm tired, and cold, and want rest. Let 's drop home memories for a moment.

RICHARD MARDYKE

I 'm afraid I 've dropped them too much already.

MADDEN

Very likely, but our adventures first. Have you any idea what kept us so long?

REFSTEIN

Pshaw! A broken wheel!

Madden

Only! May the good Lord deliver me from the phlegmatic! Here we 've been sitting in the hood of that lumbering old stage—a perfect ark on wheels—listening to swearing we could n't enjoy, by the driver and his man—outrider—or whatever you call him.

Richard Mardyke

The Zagal, I suppose.

Madden

Yes, if a bad name will hang him here. All we saw of his usefulness was his ability to get drunk on red wine out of a greasy skin which he seemed to consider a feat. Red wine! The cold wind blew down our backs and Refstein drank all the brandy. But it seems good to see you again. You never change.

Richard Mardyke

This air. The roads are still bad. I crossed a week ago myself.

Madden

Infernal. I would have gone south by Hendaye and come up from Zaragoza had I known.

Richard Mardyke

Not much longer, either—except fleas.

Madden

Don't speak of it. We were eaten alive! (*Pointing through window.*) There, Refstein, that's the view of the Maladetta I told you of—but what a fire! Are you trying to denude the land of timber?

Refstein

To Richard Mardyke

I suppose you've climbed it?

Richard Mardyke

Naturally. Over the glacier. You two
can try it if you like.

Madden

I ! I climb snow mountains and glaciers !
Gad ! It makes me feel colder than that
infernal coach. (*Drinks.*)

Richard Mardyke

Well it 's worth the climb—one of the
finest sights I know. You feel like a baby
up there. Every sound is an inspiration.
I remember once on Oroël, near Jaca, I
had started in the early morning——

Madden

Yes, I know, five A.M. on a mule—with a
boy and a stick for jabbing and shrieking
anda, anda-a-a-a ! I was in bed weeks.

RICHARD MARDYKE

Did you good! I worked my way up over the spurs of the great stone giant stretched out with his face down the valley of the Aragon. You know how he lies.

MADDEN

Looking toward the Basques.

RICHARD MARDYKE

Yes. About noon I came out on the top. Jaca lay far below, a mere gray disc on the face of the valley. The silver thread of the river glistened out of sight between the bare foot-hills. And behind was the broken mass of the Aragonese range with the highway winding through it like a white snake, here and there marked by a huge cart and ten dots one after another for mules. I was taking it all in with a sort of deep breath, running my eyes along the opposite Pyrenees wall by Canfranc towards Panticosa when of a sudden I heard a rush in the air behind me. I looked up, and a magnificent mountain eagle swept past. He was not fifty feet away. I could see his wing feathers flutter and hear the whistle of the wind over him. For a moment, as he rose out of the shadow of the mountain, and the force of the gale struck him, he seemed to pause on the very edge of the cliff as though hesitating. Then, suddenly half turning his head toward me, he slanted his great body and shot out into the abyss. It brought the tears to my eyes.

MADDEN

After a pause

Yes, I suppose so, but I prefer my eagles stuffed. Splendid for decoration. I tell you what it is, my dear fellow, modern life and mountain eagles are out of harmony— decidedly. It's my opinion that you should be back in civilization for a time. You need it. Why, everybody's inquiring about you. I live in a sort of reflected glory because I happen to know you. The old frumps with marriageable daughters were on your trail just before I left.

RICHARD MARDYKE

So much in demand as 'that! (*Laughing. It has grown dark and* NITA *enters with lights. Sound of thunder outside.*)

MADDEN

Is that thunder? (*They listen.*)

RICHARD MARDYKE

I did n't hear it.

REFSTEIN

Nor I.

MADDEN

You forget you have just inherited your uncle's fortune. Who could help loving a man with four thousand a year.

RICHARD MARDYKE

And so you marry me off? Your old trick.

MADDEN

Why not? The creed of *Mater-familias* is written between the columns of debit and credit.

RICHARD MARDYKE

And my personal attraction? (*Standing up and looking at himself.*)

MADDEN

Absolutely nothing. Why, you 're not even bald. (*Turns to* REFSTEIN, *who has lighted a cigar and sits watching the Maladetta.*) Eh, Refstein? Come, man, (*finishes his glass*), don't you think Mardyke should marry?

REFSTEIN

It would certainly be in harmony with things at present. (*He does not turn round.*)

RICHARD MARDYKE

Puzzled

At present! How in harmony with things at present?

MADDEN

Ah, that 's Refstein. He must talk. Here I 've scarcely finished that brandy

and he's getting so impatient to talk
about himself he can hardly sit still.
What's the matter with the mails here,
anyway?

RICHARD MARDYKE

Come, drop nonsense, and tell me about
your letter and give me news. What is
my mother here for?

REFSTEIN

Rising and tossing his cigar away

Yes, Mardyke, I am impatient. Impatient to talk over what I came for. You
know me. I hate this waiting and delib-
erating. I know what I have to say.

RICHARD MARDYKE

Well? (*Looking from one to the
other.*)

REFSTEIN

Taking a letter from his pocket and handing it to Richard Mardyke

Your mother gave me this for you. Read it.

RICHARD MARDYKE

Taking the letter. Opens and reads to himself. At first smiles

Dear old mother. (*Reads on. Starts.*) Geraldine! Marry! (*Reads on. Again starts. Lets his hand fall at his side.— Aside.*) To him! (*Stands for some time with his head bent down, the others watching anxiously. After some time* REFSTEIN *speaks.*)

REFSTEIN

Richard—I——

RICHARD MARDYKE

Interrupting without moving

You love—Geraldine?

REFSTEIN

Yes.

RICHARD MARDYKE

And she loves you?

REFSTEIN

I believe—she———

MADDEN

Naturally—naturally———

RICHARD MARDYKE

Aside

Only a year! (*A pause.*)   Is this what you came to discuss?

REFSTEIN

Yes—your mother———

RICHARD MARDYKE

Only a year! It is only a year since Martha———

REFSTEIN

I did not think——

RICHARD MARDYKE

You did not think I would speak of it?

REFSTEIN

You knew—we were not happy.

RICHARD MARDYKE

Yes—I *did* know—(*Suddenly.*) I know *you*—(MADDEN *rises and suddenly seizes his arm.*)

REFSTEIN

Richard, don't let us quarrel. . . . I love your sister.

MADDEN

Hopelessly

What more can a man do? (*Drinks.*)

RICHARD MARDYKE

Aside

God knows what a life she led !

REFSTEIN

Martha and I were——

RICHARD MARDYKE

You lived together five years !

REFSTEIN

Yes.

RICHARD MARDYKE

And then one of you took the affair into her own hands and you found her——

MADDEN

Rising

Stop ! I will not have this. Martha is dead. Let her rest. I can hardly respect this in you, Mardyke. (*A pause.*)

RICHARD MARDYKE

You are right, Madden. But why do you come here ? My consent is hardly wanted. It is absurd. (*Thunder.*)

REFSTEIN

You will give it, Richard ? (*He holds out his hand.*)

RICHARD MARDYKE
After a pause taking it

There was no use in the trip here. Let the past lie. (*A sudden flash of lightning. Thunder.*)

MADDEN

A good night for the discussion of love and marriage ! Look at the mountain. (*Points.*) It is white with light.

REFSTEIN

The flashes are incessant on the snow ! (*A loud peal. They go to the window.*

RICHARD MARDYKE *stands thoughtfully by the table.*)

MADDEN

What a night! Look at those white lines on the mountains. I see them flash.

RICHARD MARDYKE

Aside

White lines! Where? (*He goes toward the window.*)

REFSTEIN

The mountain is alive! There are silver threads shooting out from under the snow.

RICHARD MARDYKE

Silver threads! Where? (*They point.*) That must be water! (MADDEN *points.* RICHARD MARDYKE *hurriedly gets a nightglass and adjusts it.*) You 're right— Madden, you 're right. There will be trouble. The valley may be flooded—there are hundreds of people.

REFSTEIN

Can we do nothing?

RICHARD MARDYKE

Follow my finger. There! Do you see? That is the village. The water comes down from the height above. If it turns they may be swept away. These people will stand on the edge of destruction until it fairly runs over them.

MADDEN

There is nothing can be done?

RICHARD MARDYKE

I don't know. (*The storm increases steadily.*)

MADDEN

Look! Look! Is that water there too? Why, the whole valley is full of it.

RICHARD MARDYKE

Resting night-glass on window edge

No, not all, but all along the centre
there is a black mass running. I can see
it flash in the lightning. (*A flash.*)
There ! I saw it distinctly.—Here—take
the glass. (*Runs to opposite side of room
and takes hat and coat.*)

MADDEN

What are you going to do ?

RICHARD MARDYKE

I am going down to get a closer look at
the edge of the town. I may be able
(*picks up lantern*) to do some good
(*strikes a light and lights lantern.*)

[*In the meanwhile* PEPE *and a woman
hurry across the stage in the storm and take
refuge under the porch.* PEPE *is breathless
and covered with mud.*]

PEPE

I cannot stay, Señora. I must go back.
I will call the Señor. You can say what
you want. He will not let any harm
come. He is good, Señora. (*Is about
to knock.*)

MARTHA

Restraining him

You say there are strangers—

PEPE

Yes, Señora, two. They came up this
afternoon. They were on the coach
which was delayed. But I must knock.
(*He goes toward the door, which at this
moment opens, and* RICHARD MARDYKE
comes out, closing it behind him.)

RICHARD MARDYKE

Thank God for a breath of air. (*Running against* PEPE.) Hello ! Who 's

this ? (*Raises lantern.*) Why, Pepe!
What's the matter—the water ? Has it
come up ? I saw it in the valley from my
window here, and am coming down. Do
you need me ?

PEPE

No, no, Señor ! Thank you, and God
bless you for it.—No, the water has gone
over below, and we're safe ; but I must
go back. . . . It may turn. But there's
a young woman here to see you. I must
go, sir. She wants to speak to you.

RICHARD MARDYKE

A woman ? Where ? Who is she ?

PEPE

I don't know, Señor. She is over under
the porch. But I must go, Señor—the

water ! . . . God bless you, Señor . . .
God bless you. (*Exit.*)

RICHARD MARDYKE

A woman. (*Raises light and throws it
upon porch, disclosing figure.*) Who is
this ? . . . Can I——?

MARTHA

Gently

Richard——

RICHARD MARDYKE

Who is it—what do you want ?

MARTHA

Richard——

RICHARD MARDYKE

*Starts, throws light on the face. Martha drops
the shawl from her shoulders and stands in
the light of the lantern. He springs back.*

Good God ! Who is it ? Speak. Who
is it ?

MARTHA

O Richard . . . it is I . . . Richard!
Richard—help me for God's sake.—It is I
—Martha—don't you hear? Martha——

RICHARD MARDYKE

Martha!

MARTHA

Yes—yes—it is I, Martha. Oh, don't
stand there like that. It was not I—
it was the other—my maid that was
drowned. I had given her my clothes—
they mistook her—it was so long after—
(*Comes near him.*)

RICHARD MARDYKE
Retreating

Martha! Martha! (*Suddenly dropping
lantern with a crash, and staggering
against porch*) Oh, my God!

REFSTEIN

Inside

What was that, did you hear a fall of glass?

MADDEN

Looking out

No. Absurd! The storm rattling the window. Look at that! (*They look out. A flash of lightning.*)

MARTHA

Outside. Seizing him by the arm

It *is* true! It is I. Oh, Richard—look at me—touch me—see—I am come as I promised. Don't you remember? Oh, dear—see—— (*Sinks down at his feet.*)

RICHARD MARDYKE

Suddenly seizing her. Drags her to the light of the window by the door. Holds her for a moment in the light

Martha! (*Throws his arms frantically about her.*)

Martha

I came to you as I promised.

Richard Mardyke

As you promised! What is it all? I am blind—but you are cold. Your clothes are wet. I thought—(*stops and stands thinking*)—and *he* in there!

Martha

I have been concealed; living secretly —hide me—these men in there. Who are they?

Richard Mardyke

Yes—yes—here, come, come—quick. (*Leads her to the foot of the stairs on the porch.*) Go up there. It is my study. There is everything—fire. Stay, let me think. My head is splitting. Lock the door on the other side of the room and leave this one ajar—quick—I must go back. (*She starts away but he holds her*

a moment. Releases her.) Go quickly—
and quietly—wait for me. I will come
when I can. Quick—no noise—lock the
door. (*Kisses her hand. She goes
quickly up the stairs and stops at the top.
A flash of lightning shows her standing
there. He looks up at her and stands a moment ; then hurriedly goes to the door and
pushes it open, picking up the lantern as
he goes. Enters.*) Well (*shaking himself*),
still watching the storm? What a night.
(*Stamping.*) Just look at that lantern !

[*Curtain.*]

II.

II.

*Three hours later. Richard Mardyke's
library. Fire burning. Martha on bear-
skin divan before it. Moonlight shining
through window. Library large and
dark. Two doors: one to main house
(R.) and one to porch and stair (L.).*

MARTHA

Half rising from divan

How my head throbs! . . . like a
great hammer beating on lead . . .
beat—beat—beat. It will burst. (*Rises
and goes slowly to window. Stands in the
moonlight.*) . . . How white and still
it is! The valley is sleeping after the

struggle. . . . This crowns the memory of the storm . . . were it not for that restless scud across the moon one might forget it . . . will he never come ? . . . When I came along that road to-night the lightning was flaring in my face at every step. It leapt down into the pools and ran along the half-filled ruts. I can see the old man's shape standing out black before me. . . How my face burns ! (*The clock strikes twelve.*) More than three hours ! . . . What can keep him ? (*Throws herself down on divan again.*) . . . Who were those men ? . . . He seemed anxious to get back to them. The little man who brought me here said they came in the afternoon. . . . Oh, I am so tired ! (*A pause. Then the sound of voices in the corridor. She starts up, listens, then quickly goes to the house door*

*(R.) and stands there.   The voices come
nearer.   She slips the bolt.)*

MADDEN

In drunken voice in corridor

Never mind the light—old boy—we're
all right.

MARTHA

Startled

I know that voice! *(thinks)*—why it's
Madden!—Madden!—Madden here!

REFSTEIN

*Suddenly striking against the door and sliding
his hand over it*

What's this?—a door!—see here,
Madden.

MARTHA

*Starts back from the door and retreats to the
middle of the room trembling*

His voice! My God!

REFSTEIN

Tries the door

Well, this seems to be the end of the
hall.

MADDEN

A sound of falling

Oh, damn the hall! I say, call up Richard. Let's have a light in this hole. Hey!
Mardyke!

MARTHA

Terrified.   Goes and blows out candles

Both here!

RICHARD MARDYKE

Coming, coming. Look out for two
steps down.

MADDEN

Yes—I—I found them. Say, Refstein,
is that door locked?

REFSTEIN

Yes.

MADDEN

Suppose it's his seraglio.

RICHARD MARDYKE

There (*laughing*). Hello, Madden! Get up off the floor, old boy, and I'll show you the way.   This is B. without S.

MADDEN

I'm not drunk . . . Refstein's drunk.

RICHARD MARDYKE

Laughing

Yes, Refstein's drunk, of course he is.

MADDEN

That's what I said.   Course he's drunk.

Richard Mardyke

Come along, Refstein. Leave that door. You 're trying to break into my library.

Refstein

Madden says it 's your seraglio. (*Laughing.*)

Richard Mardyke

Oh, does he ? (*laughing.*) Come along, Madden.

Madden

Refstein 's drunk . . . Drunk as—— (*Voice dies away.*)

Richard Mardyke

Laughing

Come along, Refstein. (*Sound dies out.*)

MARTHA

After a pause goes to the door and listens

He here ! . . . Am I too late then ?
Why is Madden with him ? . . . They
never were great friends ! . . . (*Porch
door (L.) slowly opens and* RICHARD MAR-
DYKE *enters ; he locks it behind him. She
starts.*) Richard !

RICHARD MARDYKE

Martha ! (*He comes forward im-
pulsively.*)

MARTHA

*She retreats before him and stands with the divan
between them*

No—stay where you are——

RICHARD MARDYKE

Martha——(*He advances.*)

MARTHA

No—no—no—(*retreats*)—stay there—
by the divan—(*he stops*)—I must talk to
you—you must help me—I have come to
you to help me——

RICHARD MARDYKE

Dear——

MARTHA

Yes—yes—I know—but—(*aside*) Oh,
I am choking. (*To* RICHARD MARDYKE.)
Oh, Richard I did n't know that—I thought
you were here alone——

RICHARD MARDYKE

You were by the door?

MARTHA

Yes.

RICHARD MARDYKE

And you knew the voices? Yes, of course, they came to-day.

MARTHA

Why—why are they here?

RICHARD MARDYKE

About——(*Hesitates.*)

MARTHA

Geraldine?

RICHARD MARDYKE

How did you know?

MARTHA

How did I know?—it is what I came for myself.

RICHARD MARDYKE

You!—you know?

MARTHA

Am I too late ?—am I too late ?   Oh, it
can't be !

RICHARD MARDYKE

Tell me about yourself.   Where do you
come from ? You have been concealed—
tell me for God's sake.

MARTHA

I have been sitting there nearly mad—
waiting for you to come.

RICHARD MARDYKE

Oh, Martha—what does it all mean ?
(*He looks for an answer. She remains
silent.*) Why have I been blinded and
deceived.   Why have you made me mad
with all these months without a word ?—
I——

MARTHA

Richard—listen to me—I will tell you the story of these last three years—shall I?—(*He waits expectantly. A pause.*)—Do you remember the night you went away?——

RICHARD MARDYKE

Do I remember it?

MARTHA

You said to me : " I am going. I have strength to fight. . . ." I looked up at you and wondered if it were true. I thought : " He will come back."

RICHARD MARDYKE

Three years ago !

MARTHA

Yes.

Richard Mardyke

And he?

Martha

Oh, at first there was no great change.

Richard Mardyke

And then?

Martha

Later, yes. You know how miserable
everything was. It grew worse. Everything grew so hard. . . . But don't
let us waste words. I come with a pur-
pose (*hurriedly*). Listen. You remember Anna?

Richard Mardyke

Yes . . . indistinctly. That tall
woman who used to come to the house?

MARTHA

I found a friend in her. She helped me. I turned to her. She was all I had.

RICHARD MARDYKE

All ?

MARTHA

Yes—all (*hesitating and looking towards him*)—at least all I could call upon. She was so good to me !

RICHARD MARDYKE

God bless her !

MARTHA

I thought of you as fighting and winning. I said " He will win—he will train himself to forget me." That made me miserable.

RICHARD MARDYKE

Forget you! Dearest.

MARTHA

It grew fearful at times. He hated me. One night I think I was half crazed. I walked out of the house and wandered about the streets for hours. I had a half vague consciousness of taking a train somewhere and then Anna's astonished face. It all came back to me afterwards. I begged her to conceal me, to save me; not to let me go back. Fever came and I lay a week in a half conscious state dimly aware of Anna's eyes and the pain in my head.

RICHARD MARDYKE

She kept the secret?

MARTHA

Yes. But as soon as I was able she began insisting on my return. The papers

were full of my disappearance.   She was
anxious.   I felt I was placing too heavy
a responsibility upon her.   One morning
—it was the morning of the tenth day—I
saw her taking the paper away quietly.   I
of course insisted, and saw it.   You know
what I found !

RICHARD MARDYKE

The story of your death ?

MARTHA

Yes.

RICHARD MARDYKE

But how ?   Of course, I read it.   But
how could it happen ?

MARTHA

A mere chance .   .   . a girl who had
worked for me.   I had given her one of
my dresses.   No one knew it.   The body
was mangled.   Every one was deceived.

RICHARD MARDYKE

And you let them remain so?

MARTHA

Was it wrong? Oh, Richard, think—
think what it meant to go back. Even
Anna saw—She fought the idea, but she
knew! What harm could it do? I asked,
He will be only happy. There was no
one to come between—I felt free—just
think, Richard!—free! no one owned me!
I could let the love in me rise up and go
out to all things and it was not met by
something that choked it, sent it back to
grow to poison in my heart. My soul
walked outside my body and dabbled in
the pools of sunshine, leaving the poor
lagging thing floundering blindly behind.
You know, dear.

RICHARD MARDYKE

Yes, I understand.

MARTHA

I was waiting—a month passed. Another—many. I scarcely knew for what, I only knew that I was happy in that intense, wonderful freedom, when I thought of you. I said: "No, I will not come in between his life again. He will forget it all, perhaps—perhaps." Did you—did you?

RICHARD MARDYKE

You think so?

MARTHA

Tell me—tell me so.

RICHARD MARDYKE

I can tell you that I love you.

MARTHA

Then I saw your book, and I felt I had been right. I saw more clearly.

Richard Mardyke

It was the story of my life.

Martha

And of mine—at least the best of mine.
Oh, when I saw how you had lived over
and over again all those wretched hours
and days.   When I saw the whole story
all told in cold, black lines, I knew—I felt
I knew.   I could see you then.   It all
came to me again—the struggle.   I must
go.   I talked with Anna.   I asked
her a thousand questions.   A little while
ago your other book was brought.   She
gave it to me.   Then I saw the truth.

Richard Mardyke

That last was desperate.

Martha

Yes.   You wrote the past, and in this
you told me what you hoped for the
future.   .   .   .   Hopeless.

RICHARD MARDYKE

The end of the century is hopeless. The critics said it had a depressing tone. It was morbid.

MARTHA

Still I hoped you would be happy. I waited. There was only one black thing —the one chance. She saw it . . . it has come.

RICHARD MARDYKE

What chance?

MARTHA

Do you not see? . . . Geraldine. Richard, I have come here to plead with you . . . if you like—what can I do?—only you can help me.

RICHARD MARDYKE

I—how?

MARTHA

Don't you see? I have had a breath of almost happiness. I am weak. Oh, I am a coward—anything—but don't let me go back. See, I have come into your life again, out of the dark. I have fought myself so that the love you had for me might die, but your sister—— Can you not stop it and save me?

RICHARD MARDYKE

I don't know. (*Advances and seizes her. She shrinks from him, but he holds her in his arms.*) Martha—dearest. (*She suddenly throws her arms about him. He kisses her passionately. A long pause in which he watches her face.*)

MARTHA

Will you—can you?

RICHARD MARDYKE

Suppose——

MARTHA

Well ?——

RICHARD MARDYKE

Oh, Martha, I love you enough to commit a crime.

MARTHA

A crime ! Is it a crime then ?

RICHARD MARDYKE

Think !

MARTHA

She looks at him intently for a moment. Her expression changes. She seizes his arm tightly

Richard—do you mean ?

RICHARD MARDYKE

We are alone. No one knows.

MARTHA

To let—

RICHARD MARDYKE

Why should *they*? Can we not be
enough to each other? Oh, Martha,
dearest, you are everything. You are
my life—the best. See, you will be free.
Always! Think of it!

MARTHA

Aside

Free!

RICHARD MARDYKE

Holds her close to him

I cannot give you up. No. This is
the last! We are here—we are for each
other. Oh, Martha, you have left the
world, you are dead. I have been dead
these years. Think, we are forgotten already!

MARTHA

Aside

Dead! Forgotten!

RICHARD MARDYKE

No one will suffer. The punish-
ment or the happiness is to us. What
harm do we do?

MARTHA

True, what harm! (*Speaking before
her.*) What harm?

RICHARD MARDYKE

I love you——

MARTHA

What harm! . . . His face comes up
before me. I can keep from him. What
does it all matter! (*Suddenly starting.*)
But Richard . . . Geraldine . . . we have
forgotten.

RICHARD MARDYKE

I love you——

MARTHA

No—no—Geraldine. (*He tries to draw her head down.*) You must hear me—you must. Think! She is your sister. You love her.

RICHARD MARDYKE

I love you.

MARTHA

No—no. O, God, give me strength. (*Tears herself from him.*) Richard, you must listen. There is only one way. Go back with them. Go to your sister. Break up this marriage. Do it without my name, if you can. If not, do not try to conceal it. Accept it. Let him free himself of me. I shall then be really free.

Do this, dear.   Oh, dearest—will you?
Will you?

RICHARD MARDYKE

After a pause

You are right.   Yes, I will do it.

[*Curtain.*]

III.

III.

Church. Decorations of flowers for wedding. Door (R.) to vestry; door (L.) to street. Mrs. Schreiner near altar looking at flowers. Scene, Newport.

MRS. SCHREINER

Well, I suppose they won't find fault with that! (*She names various flowers of the season and comments on them.*) It will be a success so far at least. Madden said he would be here at two to tell me about Dick. He's in such a state about him! Poor boy! Back here after all this time, and to be taken down. (*Enter* MADDEN.) Ah, Tom! just thinking of you. (*Shakes hands.*) So glad to see you back. How is he?

MADDEN

Better—much better. Had a good
night and is perfectly quiet. Not a bit of
fever. All he wants now, Dr. Waldon
says, is perfect rest.

MRS. SCHREINER

And when can we go to see him?

MADDEN

Not for four or five days yet. Positive
orders.

MRS. SCHREINER

Not even Geraldine? (MADDEN *shakes
his head.*) Oh, that's too bad. She will
have to go then, after all, without a word.
It will be such a disappointment. You
know Dr. Waldon almost promised it.
But I'm so glad he's safe at last. I felt
so unsettled about the whole thing. Really,

one could n't be sure whether we would have a wedding or a funeral.   Poor Dick ! And not a soul has seen him but you.

MADDEN

Luckily I was there.   He was taken just as we left the steamer in New York. Turned white and went down on the deck all in a minute.

MRS. SCHREINER

So Margaret wrote me.   And they say you came on that night by the boat. Was n't that a great risk ?

MADDEN

He would have it.   High fever ; there was no talking to him.   By the time we reached here he was perfectly delirious. As the family did not expect him—and at such an hour—you know when the boat

gets in—I just took him to my own house
and sent for Waldon. After that, of course,
there was no moving him.

MRS. SCHREINER

Has he been very low ?

MADDEN

About as near the edge as he could go
and not topple over. Twenty-seven days
of delirium is no joke.

MRS. SCHREINER

Twenty-seven days !   ·

MADDEN

Waldon almost said there was no chance
from the first. But his constitution is like
a stone. You might pound and pound on
it and only raise the dust.

MRS. SCHREINER

Changing the position of a wreath

He always was strong. Do you remember when he took the Stone Lodge gate with that English hunter of his and galloped down the shore for hours after Geraldine?

MADDEN

Yes, and was out all night in a catamaran that broke in half, and had to be picked up in the morning, looking like a drowned rat. But it's that hermit life in Spain that has given him his chance here.

MRS. SCHREINER

Well, the cloud is cleared from Geraldine's wedding at least. Have you seen her?

MADDEN

Yes, an hour ago. I go over every day to report to her mother about Richard. Poor old lady, she's been nearly frantic.

MRS. SCHREINER

I should think so.

MADDEN

Enter Romverton with scarf about throat and Mrs. Margaret Romverton

Hello, Rom. and Margaret!

MRS. ROMVERTON

The first glimpse of you ! But I forgive it. How is he?

MADDEN

All right. Not a bit of danger. But I wrote you all about it. When did you get back?

MRS. ROMVERTON

To-day—this morning—for the wedding, of course.

ROMVERTON

To Madden

They say you 've turned nurse, old man.

MRS. ROMVERTON

De Kale has been telling me wonderful tales of your sitting up the nights together.

ROMVERTON

Got it straight from the doctor.

MRS. ROMVERTON

And you (*to* MRS. SCHREINER) arranging flowers! Was there ever a wedding that you did n't have a hand in? But it is beautiful, is n't it? (*They walk away, talking.*)

ROMVERTON

Does Dick know anything of the wedding?

MADDEN

Not a word. No excitement, you know.

ROMVERTON

Yes, of course. Poor boy! To wake up with a new brother-in-law! I saw Refstein, by the way, this morning—looked as happy as they make 'em. Might be his first, to judge by his face. Some men never learn anything by experience.

MADDEN

No, I suppose not. (*Thoughtfully glancing at* MRS. SCHREINER.)

ROMVERTON

But, I say, old man, what a lucky thing you got away from Spain before the cholera broke out, wasn't it?

MADDEN

Indifferently

Cholera ! Has it broken out there !

ROMVERTON

Yes ; fearful, they say. Hundreds dying.
Oh, and that reminds me ; you know Faldon ?

MADDEN

Faldon ? Yes, of course.

ROMVERTON

Well, he 's out there. Went a few days
ago. Had a letter from him. Says he
has a sure germicide for cholera. I suppose we 've seen the last of him. Con-
found my neck. (*Strokes it.*)

MRS. ROMVERTON

Coming up and overhearing

Yes, I should think so. There, pat it,
and cajole it. Went off for a day's fish-

ing at Montauk! Only just back! Two
weeks! Look at him! See that neck!
For a wedding! (ROMVERTON *strokes it
gently.*) Hanging for hours over the side
of the *Phantom.*

ROMVERTON

Aside

Asleep!

MRS. ROMVERTON

And not *a* fish.   Not one!   (*Turns to*
MRS. SCHREINER.)

ROMVERTON

Aside, contemptuously

Fish! (*Looks at his watch.*) But, I
say, we must go. We sha'n't have time to
get to the house and back. Come, Margaret. Do you go with us, Mrs. Schreiner?

MRS. SCHREINER

Coming up

Yes. (*Looking back.*) Is n't it beautiful! I 'm satisfied. Are you pressed for time, Mr. Romverton?

ROMVERTON

Yes, not a minute. The ushers will be upon us before we can escape. Good-bye, Tom—for half an hour.

MRS. ROMVERTON *and* MRS. SCHREINER

In chorus

Good-bye! (*Exeunt.*)

MADDEN

Good-bye. Good-bye. (*Leans thoughtfully against a pew-back. Looks at his watch*). In a few minutes they will begin to come. . . . A few minutes . . . and Richard! . . . (*Starts up.*) Oh, what in God's name does it all mean? . . . I am at sea . . . nothing certain . . . mere suspicion. A word, a cry. I have been by his bed night and day, trying my best to understand. There is no connection. . . . Nothing . . . only the one horrible thing . . . *Is* there something? What can I do? . . . or say? . . . A man in delirium! . . . They knew he loved her. They say in fever the memory brings back forgotten things. . . . But he speaks as though it were yesterday! (*Walks up and down.*) Here it is, within minutes of the end, and I stand like an infernal fool. (*Detective enters.*)

DETECTIVE

Ah, I beg pardon, is Mr. Madden——?

MADDEN

That is my name. You wish to see me?

DETECTIVE

If this is Mr. Madden (*takes out a letter*) this letter will explain. I followed you here from Mr. Mardyke's.

MADDEN

Tearing it open

At last! You are the detective then?

DETECTIVE

Yes, sir.

MADDEN

And the woman?

DETECTIVE

The French maid employed by the Countess Refstein, Marie Girot,—shall I talk to you here, sir? (*Looks about.*)

MADDEN

Yes. Tell me quickly. What have you found?

DETECTIVE

Takes out note-book, glances at pages

I was directed last Wednesday to go to New London to make inquiries as to the history of this Marie Girot, who, it seems, left the service of the Countess Refstein some days before the latter was——

MADDEN

Yes, I know.   You went to New London ?

DETECTIVE

At once.

MADDEN

Well ?

DETECTIVE

I made every possible inquiry.   I found that the woman in question came to Amer-

ica some three months before taking service with the Countess.   She came with
a relative, an aunt, who died soon after
their arrival.   She served with various
families——

MADDEN

Never mind that part of her history.
After she came to the Countess ?

DETECTIVE.

That was in August.   She was engaged
on the 9th, and was there until the 29th,
—just twenty days.

MADDEN

Yes ?

DETECTIVE

At the end of that time she suddenly
left the house and did not return.

MADDEN

And the cause ?   Was there no reason
for it ?

DETECTIVE

She had received notice to leave on the
1st from the Countess.

MADDEN

She had received notice !   You are
sure ?

DETECTIVE

There is no doubt of it.

MADDEN

Well ?—where did she go ?

DETECTIVE

I am sorry to say I cannot answer you.
The woman has never been heard of
since.

MADDEN

Aside

Great God!

DETECTIVE.

I have some further information, but it merely agrees with this. There happens to have been a man—a lover. I have received his account.

MADDEN

Well?

DETECTIVE

It seems that on the night in question he had agreed to meet the woman on a dock near the house.

MADDEN

The river! An abandoned landing? Half fallen to pieces? Close to a rocky jetty.

Detective

Exactly.   It had been a usual meeting-place, it appears.   This night the man—he is a butler—went to this place and waited until twelve, but the woman did not put in an appearance.   He then went away.

Madden

And he heard nothing—since then? He made no inquiries?

Detective

The man left with the family in whose employ he was next morning.   He was away two months.   He wrote several times, but, thinking she had done it purposely, gave it up after a while.   When he came back to New York he inquired of the servants in the town house there and found out that the woman had left.   He went at once to some lodging where she was supposed to be going on the first of the preceding September, and where he himself had sent her things. She had not gone there. Then he became alarmed and instituted a search, but, as nothing was found, he gave it up finally.

MADDEN

After a pause

Did any one see her leave the house on that night ? Do you know what kind of a dress she wore ?

DETECTIVE

No. She must have left about ten by all accounts. But no one saw her go. (*Laughter outside.*)

MADDEN

What can I do ? If it is true, God help Geraldine ! There is but one thing left

. . . I must do it—yes, it must be done !
(*Enter two Ushers.*)

FIRST USHER
They shake hands

Never ahead of you, are we ?

MADDEN
To Detective

Come around to my house to-morrow
at ten. That 's all now. (*Exit Detective.*)
I say, boys, excuse me to somebody.
Will you ? I 've got to rush off—may be
detained—important business—hope to
come back in time if possible—say important. (*Waves his hand. Exit.*)

SECOND USHER

What on earth can be up ! It must
be Mardyke. (*Enter the other ushers.
They stand talking. Soon the people be-*

*gin to arrive.   The church slowly fills.
Enter* ROMVERTON.)

ROMVERTON
To an Usher

Hello ! (*Shakes hands.*) Where's Madden ? (*Enter* MRS. ROMVERTON.   *Usher
speaking aside to* ROMVERTON.)

MRS. ROMVERTON

Ah, there you are ! (*Enter* MRS. SCHREI-
NER.) I waited for you at the corner, but,
as you had n't put in an appearance, I
hurried Romverton off. He's always late,
you know.

USHER
Ending talk with Romverton

I 'm afraid it 's Mardyke.

ROMVERTON

No one has had any word.

MRS. ROMVERTON
To Usher

Hello, what are you two conspiring about ? (*Shakes hands.*)

ROMVERTON

Nothing, my dear. (*Aside*) I'm afraid Madden has had bad news from Mardyke. He has just rushed away.

MRS. ROMVERTON

About Richard! (*Catching Usher's arm.*) What is it, Will ? (*They go on one side and talk.*)

[*The procession begins. The organ plays. The minister takes his position. The service is about to begin when* RICHARD MARDYKE *staggers to the door and enters. He takes a few steps forward. He is half dressed.*]

RICHARD MARDYKE

Stop! (*Confusion. Service stops, every-body turns.*)

GERALDINE

Richard! (*He staggers slowly forward and leans against a column.*)

RICHARD MARDYKE

Geraldine! (MADDEN *comes to the door.*)

MADDEN

He has heard all and left the house. I must have been right. (*He enters the church.*)

RICHARD MARDYKE

Geraldine! . . . Martha . . . Martha. . . . is alive! Oh, Madden. . . . I . . . (*Staggers and falls into* MADDEN'S *arms.*)

[*Curtain.*]

IV.

IV.

Scene same as at first. Night. Moon-
light. Interior dark. Sentinel passes
at intervals. Pause. Martha appears
at head of the stairs with candle.
Comes slowly down and puts it on small
table. Stands by door listening.

MARTHA

Is she asleep? . . . I thought I
heard her call. (*Opens doors gently and*
listens. After a while closes it and comes
out into the room.) . . . I am always
hearing her voice! . . . It haunts
me. (*Throws herself down on lounge.*)
. . . Pepe not here yet! (*Looks at*
clock.) Two o'clock! . . . He ought
to have come an hour ago! . . .

(*The sentinel passes. She sits up, listens; goes to the window.*) Three hours to dawn. . . . Oh, this suspense is maddening. . . . To be shut up here with this thing. . . . Poor Nita ! . . . Hour after hour, day after day, and not a word of complaint. . . . Only a moan now and then ! . . . Moonlight ! It was moonlight the night after the storm when I came ! . . . How strong they are, these poor wretches ! . . . How they fight ! . . . Fight to the end. . . . That fog at the end of the valley looks like a piece of the sea. I can see waves and masses of floating ice. . . . Not a line from him yet ! . . . Only the word from Havre that he had started. . . . Could anything—— ? . . . The same questions over and over again ! . . . Oh, God, I shall go mad ! Pepe should have come. . . . Suppose he could not pass ! (*The guard passes, she starts to one side and draws the curtain about her until he has passed.*) . . . And they set a guard on us ! . . . So that we may not escape ! . . . Escape ! (*Looks after him.*) There he goes with his yellow and black uniform. . . . How the buckles catch the moonlight ! . . . Cowards ! . . . Cholera ! . . . How the very word sends a panic through these people. . . . Does *he* know ? . . . It *must* have been in the papers ! . . . And suppose he should hear and come back ! . . . Come back ! . . . No ! No ! . . . Not now ! . . . Not now ! . . . Ah, if I could but see him for a moment ! To know nothing ! . . . *Nothing !* . . . The village is full of lights ! . . . At two in the morning ! . . . The scourge is hard at work there ! . . .

Not a house without a light ! (*Puts her face close to the pane.*) How cold it all looks down there by the bridge ! . . . The cordon begins there. . . . I could fancy I saw the flash of arms from here. . . . Fifty paces apart, Pepe says. . . . How does he pass them ? . . . Oh, I am so tired. (*After a moment goes slowly across the stage towards the sofa, stopping to listen and shake her head at the door (L.) Sinks down on sofa. Sleeps.*)

OUTSIDE :

(*Enter Officer followed by soldier carrying lantern. Officer holds a paper. Comes forward.*)

OFFICER

Here, hold up that light. (*Reads.*) Put sentries at numbers 4, 7, and 12, and stop all passing on main highway. Send reliefs to No. 16. (*Aside.*) Did that an hour ago. (*Reads.*) Extend cordon along the stream to first houses on main road. Report. (*Folds it up.*) Good! (*Enter Guardia Civil. Salutes.*) Ah! You come from the bridge?

GUARDIA CIVIL

Yes, sir.

OFFICER

How many have tried to pass?

GUARDIA CIVIL

Fourteen, sir.

OFFICER

Since when?

GUARDIA CIVIL

Since eleven o'clock, sir. (*Sentry salutes and goes on.*)

OFFICER

My orders obeyed ?

GUARDIA CIVIL

To fire at second challenge ?   Yes, sir.

OFFICER

Any hurt ?

GUARDIA CIVIL

Two, sir.

OFFICER

Women ?

GUARDIA CIVIL

No, sir.   (*Hesitates.*)   .   .   .   A man
and a boy.

OFFICER

Glances at him

They tried to run through ?

GUARDIA CIVIL

Yes, sir. By the underbrush in the river bed.

OFFICER

Let the bodies lie. . . . A good example !

GUARDIA CIVIL

Starts

Yes, sir.

OFFICER

Tell Capt. José to send me a report every four hours. Here, that light. (*Takes out paper and pencil. Writes.*) Am ordered to close main road above village. To ensure, close mountain road on your side at once, and hold till I send you word. I will picket this end. Let no one pass. There ! (*Folding it up and handing to Guardia Civil.*) Take that

to Captain José.   Have you anything
else ?

GUARDIA CIVIL

Yes, sir.   The doctor's report.

OFFICER

Give it to me. (*Looking it over.*) Hum !
Five over yesterday.   Hell 's loose down
there !   Ah, what 's this ? . . . A line
from the doctor !   (*Goes to the light and
reads.*) Wants a pass and a guide for his
assistant, an American, from the bridge to
the town. . . . An American ! . . . By
this road, I suppose.   Here (*to soldier*),
hold it higher.   (*Writes.*) Well, there 's
his pass.   He can get the guide from
José.   What the devil do these foreigners
want at such a time as this.   (*To soldier.*)
Is that all ?

GUARDIA CIVIL

Yes, sir.

OFFICER

You may go. (*Guardia Civil salutes, turns, hesitates.*)

GUARDIA CIVIL

The . . . bodies . . . to stay, sir?

OFFICER

I said so. (*Looks around.*)   Stop! Are their names known?

GUARDIA CIVIL

José and Pablo Gomez.

OFFICER

Gomez? Gomez? (*Looks up.*) What's your name?

GUARDIA CIVIL

Ricardo Gomez, sir.

OFFICER

Ah !   The same?

GUARDIA CIVIL
Choking

My brothers, sir.

OFFICER
Huskily, after a pause

Let the bodies be taken up.

GUARDIA CIVIL

Yes, sir. . . . Thank you, sir.

OFFICER

You may go. (*Guardia Civil salutes and exit. Officer stands a moment.*) Poor devil! (*Exit, followed by man with lantern.*)

INSIDE :

MARTHA

Oh, Richard! . . . Richard! (*Wakes, sits up, and looks about her.*) Oh, I thought he was here . . . I thought I heard him talking to some one. . . . Has he told them? . . . And Geraldine? . . . Poor Geraldine! . . . (*Rises suddenly, listens, goes near the door (L.) and listens again.*) Nita must be sleeping still. . . . How still it is. . . . I cannot hear her breathing. . . . Strange, I could hear her before. . . . If she can get a few hours' rest, perhaps . . . (*Pushes the door gently open and looks in. Listens. Hesitates. Takes candle and goes slowly into the room. There is a long pause. A sharp cry. The name "Nita" is repeated. Quiet again.* MARTHA *reappears hurriedly. Closes door behind her. Walks slowly and unsteadily across the stage.*) Dead! . . . It has killed her! (*Sits down on end of sofa and buries her head in her hands.*) Oh, I am alone! . . . (*The guard crosses stage and, as he disappears, Pepe also crosses and hides in*

shrubbery below window. He taps on pane.
She does not hear at first. Then, rising.)
What was that? (*Listens.* PEPE *taps*
again.) Pepe! Yes—(*Runs to the win-*
dow and opens it.) Pepe!

PEPE

Yes, Señora. The letter, Señora. Quick.
The guard. I'll wait here. If the Señora
should wish to write. . . . (*She breaks*
open the letter quickly and he sinks down
into the shadow of the window.)

MARTHA

A telegram! From him! (*Reads.*)
All is known. I leave at once. Have
been ill. Richard. (*Repeating.*) All is
known! . . . He leaves at once. . . .
Ill! . . . (*Turning it over suddenly.*) . . .
When was it sent! (*Turning it over.*)
No date! (*Goes to window and raises it*
recklessly. The Guard appears.)

GUARD

Halting

Who goes there?

MARTHA

Shrinking back into the shadow of the curtain

What have I done! He will be dis-
covered !

GUARD

Approaching

Who goes there?

MARTHA

Suddenly appearing

What do you want?

GUARD

Shut that window. (*She closes it and
waits. Guard walks slowly on and disappears. She waits some time.*)

MARTHA

In a whisper

When was it sent? Has he started?
(*Cautiously raising window.*) Pepe!

PEPE

Yes, Señora.

MARTHA

When did you get this?

PEPE

In the afternoon, Señora.

MARTIIA

Where from? It has no date. Is there
delay?

PEPE

My brother brought it. I think it was
delayed. There has been no mail brought

in for two weeks, Señora. It might be
that long since it came.

MARTHA

Two weeks! It might be two weeks!
this morning—or only yesterday! Coming! And coming here! . . . Now!
(*Leans against window frame. Suddenly
to* PEPE.) Here, Pepe. . . . Go. Go
quickly. . . . And God bless you!
(*Closes window as he disappears. She
stands listening as his footsteps die away.*)
They know all. . . . He has told them.
There has been a desperate scene, and
he, what has *he* done? . . . and
Geraldine? can she love this man? . . .
No, no. A mere child! She does n't
know. Poor child! . . . Has he
started? Oh, when was that sent.
(*Takes telegram to light and examines
closely.*) There is a mark here. . . .

(*Very attentively.*) But it is so . . . faint. . . . (*Holds it up.*) I wonder . . . (*Becomes very intent.*) . . . (*Suddenly a shot is heard, followed by two others in quick succession.*) (*She starts; drops paper.*) Firing! What does that mean? . . . Pepe. . . . He could not get by! . . . (*Another shot.*) Oh, God! They have killed him. (*Runs to the door and stands listening.*)

RICHARD MARDYKE

He suddenly runs rapidly across the stage to the door and strikes it

Nita! Martha! Open. Open the door! (*Strikes.*)

MARTHA

Staggering back from the door

Richard! . . . (*Recovering.*) Oh, Richard! Richard! . . . He has come!

He has come!—(*Begins unbarring the
door.*)

RICHARD MARDYKE

Thank God; I am in time! Open!
. . . Open quickly!——

MARTHA

Stopping, terrified

But no. . . . No. . . . He cannot.
. . . He must not. . . . Richard! Richard! . . . I cannot open. I cannot!

RICHARD MARDYKE

Open! Open! Nita! Martha!

MARTHA

Richard!—For God's sake—Hear me!
Listen!—You must not come here—there
is death—the place is infected—cholera—
cholera—do you hear—cholera——

Richard Mardyke

Open, I say! They are following me!
Open the door—(*Strikes it.*) Nita!——

Martha

Nita is dead! Dead—do you hear?——

Richard Mardyke

I have fired at the guard. They are following me. I shall be killed. (*Voices of the approaching guards.*)

Martha

He has fired! . . . The shots! It was he! (*She begins unbarring the door. Voices draw near. Guards appear as he enters the house. He slams the door and bolts it.*)

OUTSIDE :

First Guard

As they rush on the stage

In there! (*Pointing.*) I saw him go in there.

SECOND GUARD

Then we may as well stop—and a belly-ful of cholera to him.

OFFICER

Coming up

Did he go in there?

FIRST GUARD

Yes, sir.

OFFICER

Very well, you four take positions at the sides of the house.   Fire at anything that shows itself.   Let nothing leave it alive. (*They separate.   Turning to Guard just arrived.*)   Is Mariano hurt?

GUARD

Yes, sir.—In the arm.

OFFICER

Very good. Follow me. (*Guard salutes. Exeunt.*)

INSIDE :

RICHARD MARDYKE

Standing by door and listening.   To Martha

The light! (*She puts it out.*) . . . I can hear them. (*He goes quietly to the windows and closes them. As he finishes, the Officer and Guard go off.*) There is no sign. (*Goes to window (L.) and looks cautiously out.*) No one there. (*Goes to back. Shuts window and stands a moment.*) . . . Martha! (*Comes forward towards her.*) Dearest! (*Seizes her suddenly in his arms.*) At last! . . .

MARTHA

Struggles.   After a moment

No! No! Let me go. . . . Don't touch me. . . . Oh, Richard, you are risking your life. . . . (*Frees herself. She sinks down on a chair.*) . . . The

firing ?—What was it ?   .   .   .   You are
not hurt ?   .   .   .   Tell me.

RICHARD MARDYKE

No.   .   .   .   I am weak.   .   .   .   I
have been ill.   .   .   .   You got my
line ?

MARTHA

Just a moment ago ! Pepe brought it.
He must have passed you on the way.
.   .   .   Oh, you are ill, Richard !   .   .   .
Speak to me—Tell me——

RICHARD MARDYKE

They know everything.

MARTHA

What did you do ?

RICHARD MARDYKE

I sent you a letter from Havre.

MARTHA

Yes.

Richard Mardyke

After my mother left so with Geraldine for New York, Madden and I went on together. Refstein had agreed to follow and meet us on the steamer. Something detained him in Paris and he lost it. . . . I . . . I . . am weak. . . . I ran . . . from the bridge. (*He rises and staggers. She runs forward and catches him.*)

Martha

Oh, Richard—You are hurt! . . . There! Lie down. . . . (*He half lies on the sofa.*)

Richard Mardyke

Get me some brandy from the closet. I have been ill . . . very weak. . . . (*She gets it.*) There. . . . There. . . . Are they there still? (*She cautiously opens the window shutter.*)

MARTHA

I see no one.

RICHARD MARDYKE
Rises and sits on edge of sofa

Martha! . . . Come here. . . .
By me. . . . (*He rises, staggers, re-
covers, and seizes her.*) You are mine!
. . . Mine now!

MARTHA

You are weak! Sit down. . . . I
will stay here—by you. Tell me, what
have you done?

RICHARD MARDYKE

Where was I—yes—he missed the
steamer. . . . It made no difference.
I did not intend telling him. . . . I
wanted to see my mother and father and
Geraldine together. . . . Just before

we arrived I was taken ill. . . . A
fever ! . . . I only remember insisting
on going to Newport that night. Madden fought, but we went. . . . I don't
remember any more. They took me to
his house. He was so good! Nursed
me for nearly a month.

MARTHA

And Geraldine ?—The marriage ?——

RICHARD MARDYKE

I knew nothing. The preparations had
gone on. . . . I . . . my head
throbs so ! (*Drinks.*) . . . I must
. . . have run very hard. . . . Don't
touch the light. . . . They may be
there ! (*Points.*)

MARTHA

Go on—tell me——

Richard Mardyke

I came to myself just before the marriage. . . . I asked them. . . . They lied about it. . . . They could not know I had come for that. . . . They told me the date had been changed. . . . Anything. . . . Anything to keep me quiet. . . . Fortunately Madden. . . . He had been with me all the time. . . . He had heard me rave about you. . . . I was delirious for days. . . . About the whole thing. . . . He suspected. He sent a detective. . . . About the girl . . . the French girl . . . your maid——

Martha

Marie?

Richard Mardyke

Yes. . . . Found she had disappeared. . . . He came to me . . .

just before the marriage. . . . I had
only time . . . to . . . to stop
him——

MARTHA

To stop him !

RICHARD MARDYKE

Yes. . . . The fools ! . . . To
let me lie there ! . . . Madden saw
. . . he suspected what I had come
for. At the last moment he came and
told me, and asked me to tell him the
truth. . . . I was mad. . . . I
rushed to the place. . . . The marriage was almost over. . . . Think !
. . . Almost over !

MARTHA

It was over. She?——

RICHARD MARDYKE.

They . . . I stopped them. . . . I must have fainted at something. . . . Madden told them. . . . They took me away——

MARTHA

And Geraldine?

RICHARD MARDYKE

I don't know any more. The fever came back. . . . Madden was with me day and night. . . . At last I was able to leave my room. . . . I saw no one. I came on the first steamer. Madden said he would manage it all the best he could. . . . What was that? (*The sentinel passes.*)

MARTHA

Listening

That is the guard they have put on the house.

RICHARD MARDYKE

A guard. . . . What do you
mean ?

MARTHA

Yes, to keep us from escaping. We
must not go out. Oh, Richard, Nita is
dead . . . in there. (*Points.*)

RICHARD MARDYKE

Looking about him

A guard! But we must get away!
. . . You must leave here . . . at
once——

MARTHA

Leave here! We cannot leave, Richard. Where should we go? You are
ill——

RICHARD MARDYKE

No, no. To Huesca. . . . By way
of Barbastro and the railroad. I know

every part. . . . There is no use trying to get to France. . . . We must
have animals. . . . Pepe! . . . Yes,
he can get them.

MARTHA

Oh, Richard, how could you pass the
lines? It is all he can do to come here
himself. It is impossible!

RICHARD MARDYKE

But we must go! We must, there is
death here. . . . The whole country
is full of it. . . . We can walk to
Pons. . . . There is no danger.
They could not watch the whole line
there—on the frontier it is different—but
here—I—(*Suddenly staggers onto the sofa.*)
Oh, Martha! (*She rushes to him and
holds the brandy. He drinks.*)

MARTHA

Richard ! . . . You are hurt ! . . . Your hand trembles ! (*Goes to the lamp and turns it up.*) . . . Oh ! (*Starts back again in horror. Comes and kneels by him.*) Oh, you have been playing with your life ! . . . Look ! There is blood ! (*Tears open his coat.*) Oh, dear, why did you ? . . . (*He sinks back unresistingly.*) You were wounded coming here. (*Works rapidly.*)

RICHARD MARDYKE

Nothing. . . . A mere scratch. . . I ——

MARTHA

Take the brandy . . . quick ! (*Holds it to his lips.*)

RICHARD MARDYKE

Martha !

MARTHA

Yes, dear.

RICHARD MARDYKE

Martha .   .   .   tell me you love me,
dear .   .   .   tell me .   .   .

MARTHA

Oh, yes—yes. Drink—drink—oh, what
can I do ?—What can I do ?

RICHARD MARDYKE

Takes her hand

We .   .   .   must .   .   .   leave
here .   .   .   (*gasps*) at once. (*Falls
back. His hand relaxes, dies.*)

MARTHA

She looks at him terrified

Richard ! Richard ! (*Seizing his hand*)

Richard, hear me !—Speak to me ! (*Suddenly falls down beside him and buries her face in the pillow, sobbing.*)

OUTSIDE :

FIRST VOICE

Who goes there ?

SECOND VOICE

Friend.

FIRST VOICE

Halt. (*A pause. A sound of guard examining doctor's pass.*)

FIRST VOICE

Of guard

Very good. Pass on. (*Two figures appear. Doctor—and soldier as guide.*)

DOCTOR

To soldier

Is this the house where you said there were Americans living?

SOLDIER

Yes, sir.

DOCTOR

Very well, I 'll go in.

INSIDE :

MARTHA

Suddenly rising and seizing Richard Mardyke's hand

Oh, he is not dead !—He is not dead !— This place !—Air—air—(*Rushes to a window, back, and throws it open. As she raises the sash there are two sharp reports and the glass falls in fragments.   Martha staggers slowly backwards across the stage.)* They thought it was—(*Reaches the sofa and falls across the body of Richard Mar-dyke.   Dies.*)

OUTSIDE :

DOCTOR

That was a woman's voice !

[*Curtain.*]